Fun at Grandma Sadie's
A Story For
Rosh Hashanah

By Sarah Mazor
Illustrations Benny Rahdiana

In the town of Paldore
Lives a little old lady.
The children in the neighborhood
Call her Grandma Sadie.

She has no grandkids of her own,
But one would never know.
When children visit grandma's house
Their faces shine and glow.

Grandma Sadie loves the kids.
She makes them feel so good.
She tells great stories, and she makes
The most delicious food.

Her heart is big and generous
And filled with warmth and love.
Being a grandma, though she's small,
Fits her like a glove.

To grandma's house, the kids all came
A few hours just before
The Rosh Hashanah holiday,
To learn and play and more.

"You know," said Grandma with a smile,
"It all begins tonight."
She looked inside a yellow file
At pictures colored bright.

"Every fall we celebrate
And thank God for the birth
Of our amazing universe,
Which we call Planet Earth."

Pomegranate: *Rimon*

"We can make it better yet
By doing kindly deeds.
Do as many Mitzvahs as
The number of *rimon* seeds."

Mitzvahs: *Good deeds*

"Look at this," said Grandma Sadie,
"It's in Hebrew, who can read?"
"I think I can," said little Saul.
"He can!" The kids agreed.

Saul was glad and proud to be
The first to volunteer.
"Shanah tova," he read out loud,
"A wish for a good year."

Grandma motioned, "Come to me."
She kissed Saul on his head.
"I see you're all prepared to play,
Who'll answer next?" She said.

"I'll be next, I'd like to try,"
Piped up clever Shirley.
So Grandma showed another card
With a ram's horn, long and curly.

"This horn is called a Sho-far,
Its sound is a reminder
For all the people of the world
To be good and to be kinder."

"It's also a reminder
To pray to God above,
To shower us with blessings
And with a lot of love."

"Yes my darling, you are right!"
Grandma said with pride.
She then took out two more things
From the satchel by her side.

A Shiny apple and some honey.
"What do these symbolize?
Go ahead and tell us, Donny,
Are we to bake some apple pies?"

Donny laughed and said, "That's funny."
The other kids were laughing too.
"May we have a slice of apple
With some honey, maybe two?"

"Yes," said Grandma, "but dear Donny,
First, please tell us why we eat
Juicy apples dipped in honey,
Then you all may have your treat."

"It symbolizes," said the boy,
"Our wish for a sweet new year
For all the children, big and small,
Living far from us or near."

"We also wish for all the kids
To have what we all do.
The sweetest grandma in the world,
A grandma just like you."

"Oh my sweets, I love you so."
Grandma said and wiped a tear.
"Come eat apples dipped in honey
And have a super sweet New Year."

May you be inscribed for a good year

The Grandma Sadie Guide To Rosh Hashanah Traditions

רֹאשׁ הַשָּׁנָה
Rosh Hashanah

The literal meaning of
Rosh Hashanah
is the "Head of the Year" and
the "First of the Year."

תִּשְׁרֵי
Tishrei

The Jewish new year begins in the
autumn with *Tishrei*, the first month
of the Jewish calendar.
Rosh Hashanah is celebrated on
the first and second days of *Tishrei*.

תְּקִיעַת שׁוֹפָר
TEKIAT SHOFAR / SHOFAR BLOWING

There are many reasons why a ram's horn is blown on *Rosh Hashanah* during services. The most famous is that the sounds of the *shofar* wake the heart and reminds all to do what is good and what is right.

סִימָנִים

Simanim / Symbolic Foods

The festive *Rosh Hashanah* meal includes symbolic foods that represent hopes for the new year.
Special dishes include round *challahs*, apples dipped in honey, fish, pomegranate, and new seasonal fruit.

חַלּוֹת עֲגֻלּוֹת
CHALOT AGULOT / ROUND CHALLAHS

The *Challah* is a special *Shabbat and holiday* bread. The regular *challahs* are braided, but the *Rosh Hashanah challahs* are round in shape and made sweeter. Some people add raisins to the dough. The sweet round *challahs*, which have no beginning and no end, symbolize our wishes for a sweet new year filled with many blessings.

תַּפּוּחַ בִּדְבַשׁ

TAPUACH B'DVASH /
APPLES DIPPED IN HONEY

The nation of Israel is compared to the apple tree. That is why it is an apple we dip in honey to symbolize our hope for a sweet year.

רֹאשׁ שֶׁל דָּג

ROSH SHEL DAG / THE HEAD OF A FISH

Eating the head of fish during the *Rosh Hashanah* holiday meal symbolizes our desire to be successful leaders (heads) and not followers (tails).

רִימוֹן

Rimon / Pomegranate

The *rimon* is one of the special Seven Species of Israel. It has 613 seeds, like the number of mitzvahs (commandments) in the Torah. Eating a *rimon* and its many seeds symbolizes our wish to do lots of good deeds in the coming year.

פְּרִי חָדָשׁ

PRI CHADASH / NEW FRUIT

On *Rosh Hashanah*, it is traditional to enjoy a new fruit - a seasonal fruit that has not yet been eaten - to symbolize the newness of the coming year.

(Figs are just one example)

SHANAH TOVA U'METUKAH

שנה טובה ומתוקה

A GOOD AND SWEET NEW YEAR

Made in the USA
Columbia, SC
25 September 2019